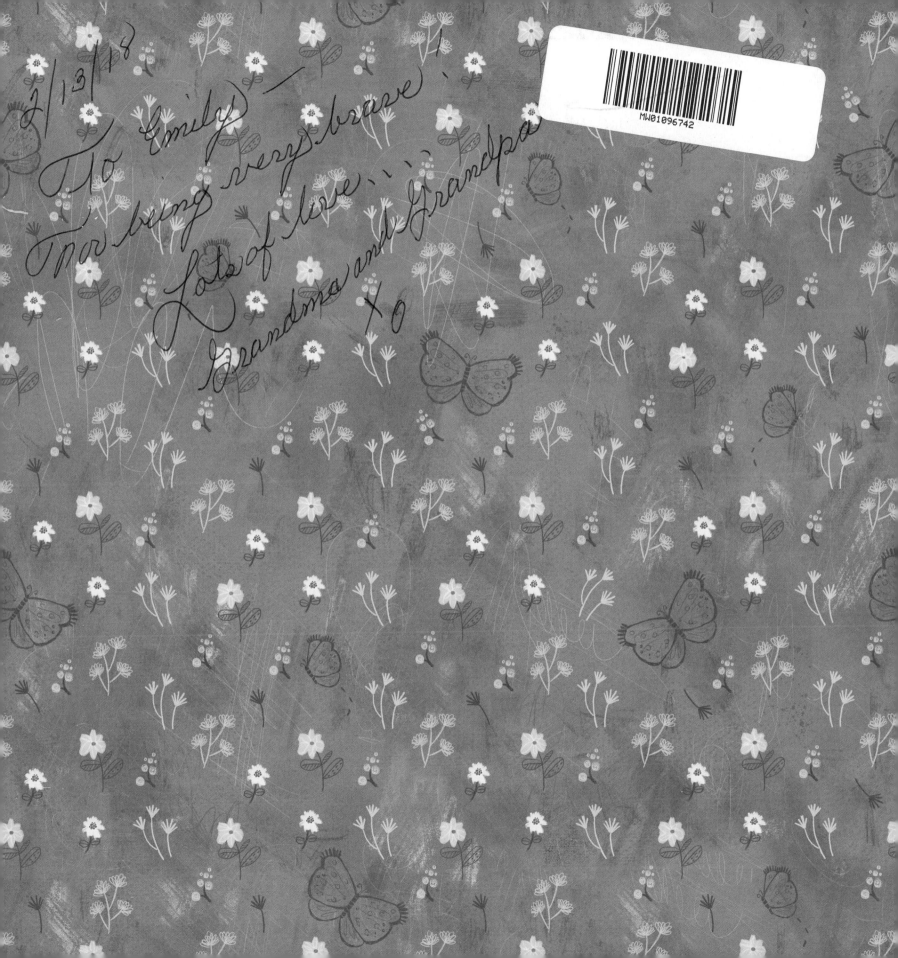

2/13/18

To Emily —
For being very brave!
Lots of love...
Grandma and Grandpa
XO

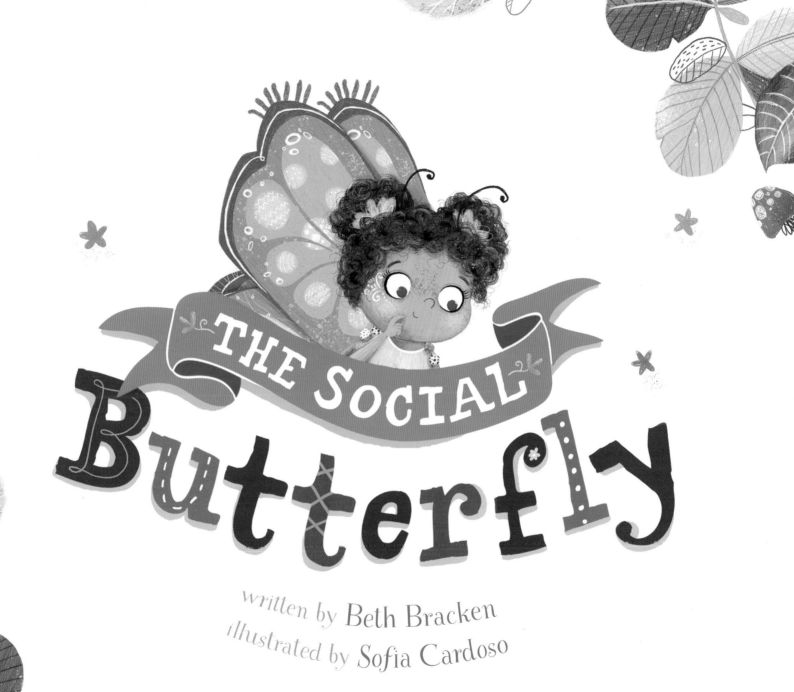

THE SOCIAL Butterfly

written by Beth Bracken

illustrated by Sofia Cardoso

PICTURE WINDOW BOOKS

a capstone imprint

The Social Butterfly is published by
Picture Window Books, a Capstone imprint
1710 Roe Crest Drive
North Mankato, Minnesota 56003
www.mycapstone.com

Library of Congress Cataloging-in-Publication data
is available on the Library of Congress website.

ISBN 978-1-5158-1697-3 (paper-over-board)
ISBN 978-1-5158-1696-6 (library bound)
ISBN 978-1-5158-1698-0 (eBook pdf)

Summary: Charlotte loves talking, singing, and playing.
What Charlotte doesn't love is sitting still, being
quiet, and listening, which is a big problem at school.
Charlotte's overly social ways interfere with her
friendships and her learning. Will Charlotte be able to
modify her behavior and learn when to be social and
when to be quiet?

Designer: Aruna Rangarajan

Printed and bound in the USA.
010751S18

For Charlotte and Etta, my two favorite chatterboxes. —BB

For my school teachers that said I chatted too much and for my friends
whose textbooks were filled with random food doodles during class. —SC

Charlotte **loved** being with her friends.

She loved playing
dolls with Lily,

dress-up
with Etta,

house
with Ben,

and trucks with Max.

And Charlotte was quite good at making new friends, too!

She made friends at the
store, at the library,
and at school.

Charlotte loved school.
She loved learning!
And she **loved** being
with her friends. But
sometimes, she tried to do
both at the **same time!**

During morning meeting, she *kind of* listened to Miss Flora, but she mostly **whispered** with her friends.

At reading time, Charlotte finished her
book. She wanted to talk with Etta.

But when she was talking, Etta couldn't read.

Then it was math time. Charlotte was one of the first to finish the worksheet. She wanted to sing with Max. But when she was singing, Max couldn't focus on adding.

And when it was lunchtime . . .

. . . Charlotte was so busy talking and laughing with Lily and Ben that none of them had **time** to eat.

That meant all
three of them were
really hungry
after recess.

The next day was show-and-share, but Charlotte didn't know that. She hadn't been paying attention during morning meeting the day before.

She didn't have anything to share.

And neither did Etta because they'd been talking instead of listening.

When Charlotte finished her book at
reading time, she started talking to Etta.

"Charlotte!" Etta cried. "I can't read when you're talking!"

After Charlotte finished the day's math worksheet, she started to tell Max a joke.

"Charlotte!" Max said. "I can't count when you're talking!"

At lunchtime, Charlotte sat between Etta and Ben.

Before she could even open
her mouth, Ben said,

"My mom says I shouldn't talk at
lunch anymore. I was so hungry
yesterday that I was kind of a handful."

During recess, Charlotte talked to Miss Flora.

"My friends don't like me today," Charlotte said.

"That's not true," Miss Flora said. "Your friends like you."

"Then why don't they want to TALK TO ME?" Charlotte asked.

"What's your favorite thing about school?"
Miss Flora asked Charlotte.

"That's easy! Reading and math
and being with my friends!"
Charlotte said.

"Your friends like those things too," Miss Flora said. "But when someone's talking to them, they can't learn!"

"I think I get it," Charlotte said.

The next day, Charlotte sat behind Lily during morning meeting. But she didn't talk. Charlotte sat **still** and **listened.**

She sat next to Etta during reading time.
Charlotte sat still and listened.

Charlotte sat next to Lily during math.
She **waited** until Lily finished her
worksheet before she told her a joke.

She ate lunch next to Ben. They talked a little, but they **finished** all of their *food*.

And when it was time to go outside, Charlotte was ready to **run**, talk, *sing*, and play.

And so were her friends!

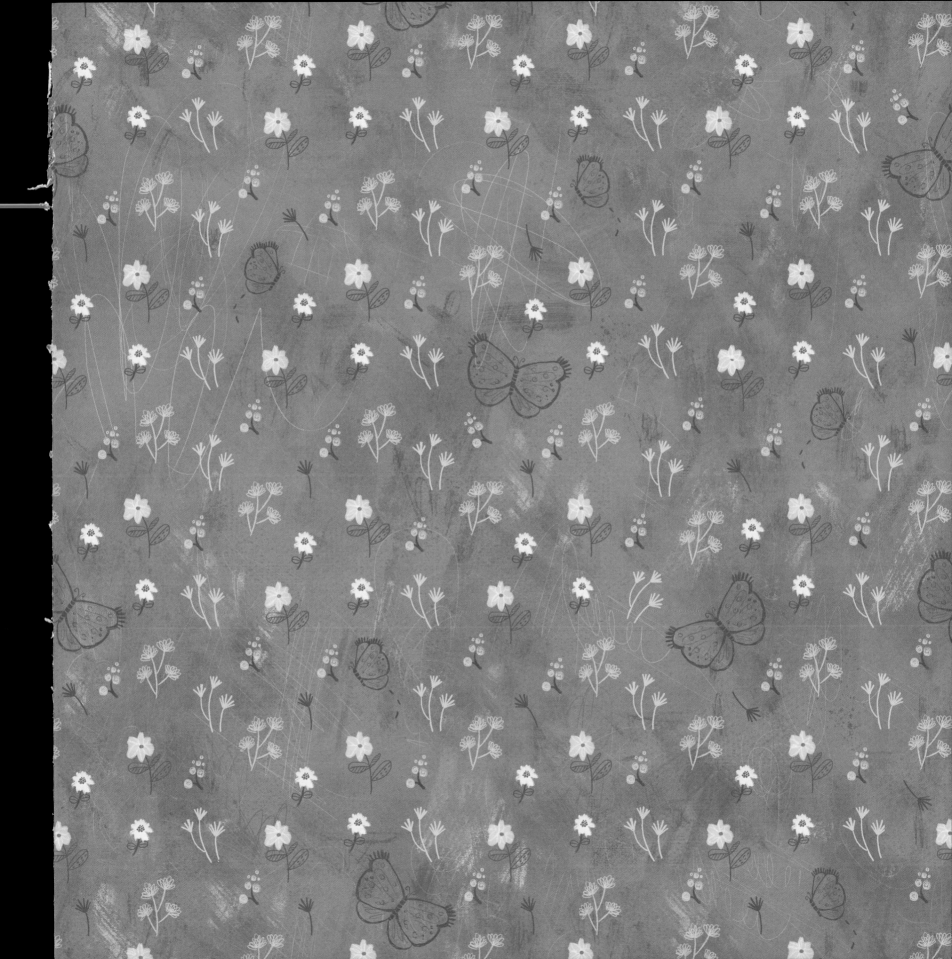

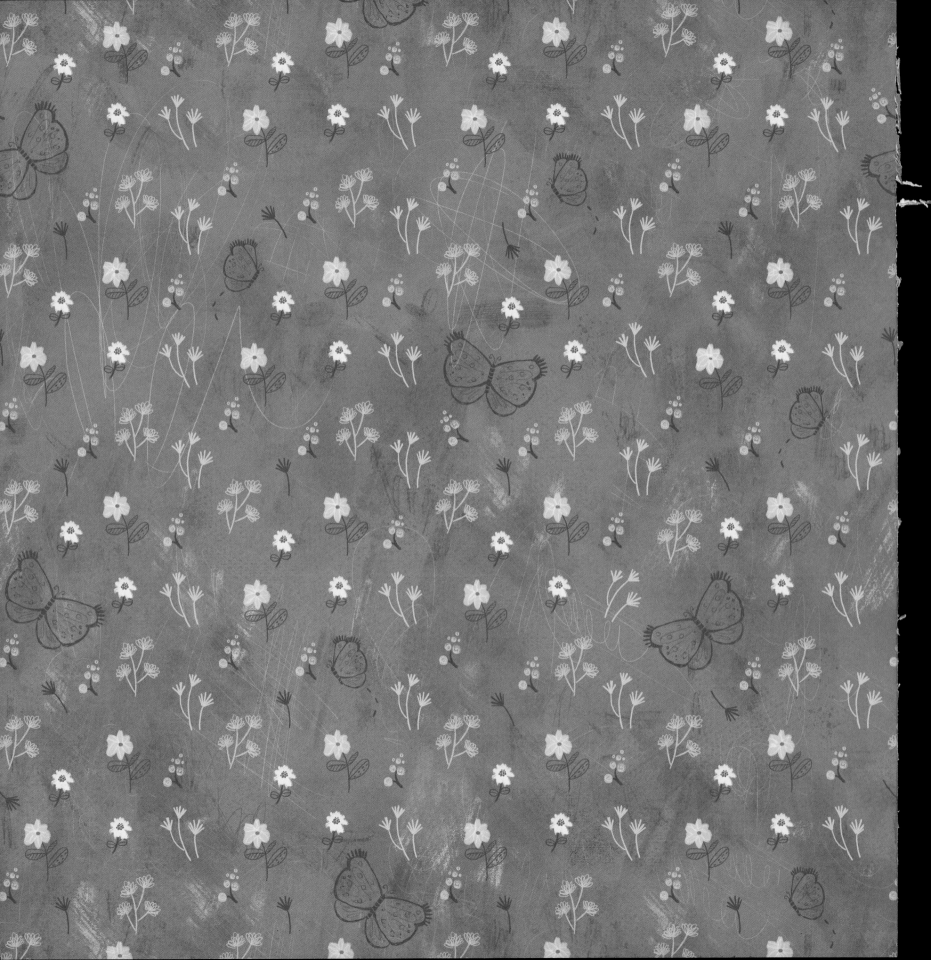